Foreword

Then I pictured our hero, he's a distinguished old man.
A grandfather - possibly a great grandfather.
He loves family and he's still a bit of a rebel, loves a
naughty irreverent story and can't resist telling his
wee fiends of things perhaps they shouldn't really
know.

He loves nothing more than to sit in his big chair, by
the fire and with a large dram in his hand, stare into
the flames and reminisce!

He loves to tease his long suffering but feisty wife,
who has a story or two of her own to tell, she also tries
to curb the excesses of his tales.

Ye Ken he's the Grand Da you always wanted.
The one you nagged for stories.
He is a hero to all the grandchildren.
So here they are:

Granny's adventures and thoughts are also included
as are several other poems written since the publication
of Totally Obsessed.

Credit is given to Diana Gabaldon - the books which
have inspired these stories and the characters are hers,

I hope I have told excerpts from her stories from a different perspective and with a poetic spin.
As always, I pay tribute to her fine writing and hope that my work in some way adds a further dimension to what she has created.
I hope that one day she may stumble across my work - and approve of it in some way. I hope I have treated her characters with the utmost respect.

Again, I thank the Facebook Outlander Fan Pages on which I have published. Those being,
Outlander Series, Books and TV and also Diana Gabaldon Fans.

They have provided, endless support, boosted morale, critiqued, provided guidance on content, and corrected punctuation and spelling. Encouraged me to keep going and along the way raised a useful amount for my two groups of Riding for the Disabled in the UK.

I also thank my RDA friends and of course my own long-suffering husband for their support.
He who has been the butt of a few poetic jokes and has resisted the temptation to burn me at the stake in our back garden!

I don't aspire to be Wordsworth or Keats - but if my efforts have raised a smile over your morning coffee, or an eyebrow or maybe a tear or two then I have done my job.

All revenue generated by my work is donated to Riding for the Disabled.
During the Covid Pandemic there has been no Riding, but the horses and ponies still need to be cared for. The charity provides valuable therapy for people of all ages with a wide range of life limiting conditions, all through the medium of horses.

Thank you.

Contents

Grand Da's Fireside Tales

Bedtime Stories

Come sit here by your Grand Da's knee
Sit quiet and verra still!
And I will tell you of my life.
Listen if you will.

I will tell you stories from
A long, long time ago
And a lifetime of adventures
Ye ken I'll tell them slow.

Put the plaid across my knees.
Keep yer Grand Da warm
Put more on the fire.
Pour Grand da a dram.

It all began back in a time.
Before my hair was white.
With the Bonnie Prince in 45
With the Jacobites.

I'll tell of Uncle Dougal,
The War Chief of the Clan
Of my godfather, old Murtagh
Exasperating man.

Of Warriors like Angus... and Rupert
All long dead.
And a funny little lawyer
I believe he was called Ned.

I'll tell of English Redcoats,
And American Revolution,
Of History and Mystery
Of fighting and confusion.

And then there is abiding love.
From family travelled far.
Tales of life on Frasers Ridge,
And how I love your dear Grandma.

Sit by me now my little ones.
And I will tell you slow,
A story Once Upon a Time
200 years ago.

✱✱✱✱

Childhood at Lallybroch

Ye see ye Grand da was born in Scotland.
Though I have travelled far,
My family farmed this land ye ken.
That would be yer great Grand Da.

I had a brother then called Willie,
That's his picture in the hall.
We got into some awful scrapes,
Had some thrashings, I recall.

Now my Da – Brian was a big man,
Hair as black as night,
Shiny like a silkie seal,
A braw, great man aright.

He could surely wield a strap,
When my arse he had tae skelp,
Much as he tried, I never cried,
He never made me Yelp.

Me and Willie let the cows out,
Took them for a ride,
Da could get no milk that day.
No matter how he tried,

One day we went down to the stream,
Collected all the toads,
And let them in the kitchen,
To make our ma scream loads.

All our misdemeanours,
Ended up with pain,
It would get a message home,
Ye'd not do that again.

See the little wooden snake,
That one upon the shelf,
My brother Willie gave it me,
He carved it all himself,

I kept him in my sporran,
It's carved with my name - Sawney,
He got stolen once in Paris.
But that's another Story.

Have ye had yer supper,
Ye little sleepy heads,
It's getting late, the fire is low.
I think it's time for bed.

****

Granny Claire

Gather a wee bit closer,
Listen if you dare,
I'll tell you a big secret,
Of your Granny Claire!

Granny Claire knows everything,
Of how tae treat your ills
With all her herbs and potions
And her little homemade pills,

When I met yer Granny
I was injured then, of course.
I'd been fighting with the redcoats.
And fallen off my horse.

She fixed my injured shoulder,
In front of all the men,
She ordered them about a bit,
She's good at that, ye ken.

My famous uncle Dougal,
He liked her by and by,
'Twas him that made me marry her,
He Thought she was a spy.

She could tell the future,
She warned us what would be.
She also had some healing tricks,
Which were very new – ye see.

She wasn't into customs,
Practiced by poor folk,
She tried to save a changeling child,
She thought fairies a joke.

I rescued her from Cranesmuir,
Getting flogged, without a stitch,
When folk had her arrested,
They thought she was a witch.

'Twas then I bid her tell me,
Truthfully ye see,
Who on earth she really was,
Before she married me.

She told me of her journey,
Through the standing stones,
From a time so far ahead,
It chilled me to the bones.

She told of what would happen.
To the Scottish Clan,
The battle of Culloden,
Would end them – to a man.

She also told of other wars,
Of battles yet to come,
Some we'd win, some we'd lose.
Of peace that was hard won.

Yer Granny Claire is old now,
Her hair is white as lime,
But she's still my brown-haired lass,
My traveller through time.

****

The Black Kirk

When I was sent to Leoch,
To learn of castle life,
When I was a teenage lad,
Long before I had a wife.

We used to go adventuring,
To the ruined Kirk
Play amongst the gravestones,
It was the devil's work.

Once occupied by men of god,
Old Nick now haunts its walls,
Us lads would give our very souls,
To hear the Devil call.

We'd run around and taunt him,
Piss upon his stones,
And eat his wild garlic,
Dance upon his bones.

Some would get away with it,
Others he would curse,
Possess their souls and take them,
To his universe.

Now remember Tamass Baxter,
He verra nearly died.
Exorcised by Father Bain,
That was all he tried.

Lying in convulsions,
Tied down to his bed,
Doomed to die by a man of god,
The last rites had been said.

Claire saved Tamass Baxter,
Found out what he ate.
Lily of the valley, not Garlic
Got him in this state.

She mixed him up a potion,
One which brought him round,
In minutes little Tamass
Was back with us – safe and sound.

Father Bain was jealous,
His nose put out of joint,
Called her the whore of Babylon,
He had to make his point.

He turned up at Cranesmuir.
He said he'd got it wrong,
But managed to convince the folk.
She'd been a witch all along.

Bain was a dogmatic man,
You'd never call him wrong,
There was no mercy in his soul,
He didn't sing that song.

But the people loved him.
This callous polished turd.
Believing that the wrath of God
Was in his every word.

✳✳✳✳

Our Wedding

Dougal thought I married lightly,
Believed it all on paper.
Just wed her, and then bed her.
And if she complains then rape her.

But she will be mine forever.
And I tell it true.
I would make this day a special one.
If it's the last thing I ever do

I rummaged in my sporran.
In there I found a thing
The front door key to Lallybroch
That would make a ring.

I married as a Fraser.
I am ready – Je suis prest.
And I married in my Tartan.
Not Mackenzie on that day.

And we were married by a priest.
In the papist way
And in a church – before God
In Latin we must pray

My bride indeed did have a dress.
Something verra fine
to suit the Lady Lallybroch
That she'll will be now she is mine

I laid my conditions down.
To wed my Sassenach
A marriage till we both should die.
There would be no turning back.

I think I fell in love with her.
When she laid her head,
For comfort on my shoulder,
And cried, her husband – dead.

I knew she'd try and run away,
To where, I did not know.
I knew I'd do my damndest.
Not to let her go.

Outside the kirk she dazzled,
She fairs out shone the sun,
A woman far too good for me
A traitor on the run.

We hardly knew each other,
That would take a while,
But I knew she was Mo Nighhean Don
First time I saw her smile.

Marriage is a serious thing,
Do not take it light,
When you find your soulmate
You'll know that it is right.

And I know she's somewhere listening,
she can hear us through the walls,
If I don't take good care of her,
She'll surely have ma balls.

****

A Bad Day at the Office

It wasn't perhaps the best of days,
The day that I met Horrocks,
Always trust an Irishman,
To talk a load of bollocks.

What he told me was the truth,
Jack Randall did the shooting,
He took the gold, and rode away,
With Irish laughter hooting.

And that bloody stupid woman!
The one who is my wife,
Had been taken by the redcoats,
Another cause of strife.

With just Murtagh, Rupert, Angus
I rode hard for the Fort,
We had to get Claire out of there,
Jack would make her talk.

We knew the best way to get in,
The gate along the sea,
They'd used it when they came here last,
The day they rescued me.

I'd get Claire, and their big plan.
To set up a distraction,
Keep the bastards occupied,
While I sprang into action.

I heard the screams, her cry for help,
From his office in the tower,
I was climbing down the wall,
The hero of the hour.

As I broke in through the window,
Empty pistol cocked,
I caught him with his breeches down,
He did look rather shocked.

I fought hard to contain my rage,
For it may have cost my life,
I asked Black Jack so courteously,
To unhand my wife!

A knife was held up to her throat,
The pistol I surrendered,
He'd make me watch him raping Claire,
Before this ordeal ended.

I'll call his bluff, I'll try my hand,
Make him pick up the gun,
Just let him then put down the knife,
Then we'll have some fun.

I was shaking now with anger,
Or fear, or some emotion.
As Black Jack picked the pistol up,
To shoot me was his notion.

I'd not back down, I'd press my case.
And see how things unfolded,
He thought he had me in his sights,
I knew it wasn't loaded.

The powder cracked, there was no shot,
I went for the knife,
My sole intent was to free Claire,
Not to take his life.

Then I heard the powder blast,
Time was wearing thin,
We'd have to jump out, off that wall,
God, I hope the tide is in!!

****

How Not Tae Treat Yer Wife

I hope yer granny's listening.
This one may make her shout,
I'll tell ye how tae treat yer wife.
To sort her nonsense out!

Now yer granny is a feisty one,
If I leave her in a place,
When I get back, she will have gone,
And then I must give chase,

More than once her wandering
Has got her into trouble,
Captured by the Redcoats,
I must follow at the double,

She put us all in danger,
When we stormed the Fort,
We'd all be for the hangman,
If we happened to get caught.

'Twas expected of me,
To discipline my wife,
But doing it, well that would be.
The worst move of my life.

She'd vowed she would obey me,
But she must take the strap.
She will not take this lying down,
I must expect some crap.

First, she threw the pewter jug,
Then she threw the plate,
Then the vase complete with flowers,
Her throwing arm is great.

When finally, I captured her,
I pinned her to the bed,
And when I pulled her night shift up
She screamed foul words instead,

I said I'd only give her six.
If she stopped the shouting.
So, she kicked me in the heid,
And nearly caved my mouth in.

She had her six, and then six more,
And then she called me names,
She wouldn't even look at me.
She wasn't playing games.

But I love yer Granny Claire.
I'll love her past my death.
I vowed I'd not raise hands to her,
As long as I draw breath.

Girls when you have a husband.
Boys when you have a wife,
Talking is solution.
To the problems in your life.

Now up the stairs and quickly
Before I come to harm,
And granny starts to exercise.
Her deadly throwing arms.

Jamie! I heard all of that.
I'm sure I made an oath.
To cut your heart out with your Dirk
And eat it raw on toast.

****

A Man of Letters

Need a lawyer! Neds the man
To sort your legal papers
The breadth of his experience
Would give a lady vapours.

A man of education,
By books, and school of life,
From the city to the Highlands,
And he doesn't have a wife!

Qualified in Edinburgh.
He is a man of letters,
He also is a Jacobite.
Though he's avoided any fetters.

He operates from Leoch.
And rides out for the rents.
Big buddies with the War Chief!
I think they share a tent!

They have a common purpose.
Money for the cause.
Parading Jamie's flogging
To Jacobite applause.

The Lairds rent goes in one bag,
Their collection in another,
They'll be in some hot water,
If it's found by Dougal's' brother.

Ned will get off lightly,
Talk his way around,
Callum will not banish him,
There are too few lawyers in town.

So, if you need your Will writ,
Or treason is your game,
Sell your house? Divorce your wife?
Ned Gowan is the name!

He'll also source a wedding dress.
If you're really stuck.
But don't ask where he found it!
"Twas just a stroke of luck

****

Forgiveness

Yer Grand Da, lived in violent times,
We must na' be forgetting,
The Clans were always stealing kine.
Falling out and feuding,

They were days when every man.
Wore his weapons daily,
Ye kept yer dirk beside yer bed,
Hope yer wits don't fail ye.

Yer Grand Da got into some scrapes,
So did yer Granny Claire.
If one was in some danger,
The other one was there,

We both have done some foolish things,
But don't love each other less,
Bound closer ye ken because of them,
And we have forgiveness.

We both speak harshly when we're mad,
We argue and we spat,
Yer Granny ends up throwing things,
She's even thrown the cat!

But when I've dodged the crockery,
And her lashing tongue survived.
I will forgive her all of it,
For we are alive.

We always lived life day to day,
Bore hardship with a smile.
She forgave me once for duelling,
That one took a while,

When you love another,
Truly and for life
And this applies to family.
Not just to yer wife,

Forgiveness is the glue that sticks,
Learn it in your youth.
Family is bonded by.
Forgiveness and the truth.

****

Campfire Raiders

Let's walk up yon mountain.
And look down from the hill,
I'll tell ye one more story,
Before the night gets chill.

Find a place to make a fire,
Some wood that isn't damp
And a tale of when the Grants men,
Came to raid our camp.

We were out collecting rents,
And settled for the night,
Sitting round our campfire,
When the horses took a fright.

Rupert was there telling tales,
The Water horse ye ken,
I've told ye that one many times,
I won't tell it again!

We heard the horses restless,
Knew something was amiss,
Not just old Ned Gowan
Going to take a piss.

Every Clansman makes his bed.
Nor far from his sword
His dirk only a stretch away,
Can grab them at a word.

Rupert didn't take a breath,
The story he kept telling.
Hiding in the bushes,
Was trouble – we were smellin'.

With nods and winks and signals,
Prepared to fight the raiders.
Each warrior knows his place and job.
And how to kill invaders.

Out of the bushes, screaming loud.
The Grants they came a running,
Trying to steal our Wagons.
But we had heard them coming.

I was fighting back-to-back.
With Dougal – he's my kin.
A fearless warrior with a sword
My uncle won't give in.

The clash of swords, the yells of men,
The Grants were on the run,
They'd only taken one poor horse,
When Ned Gowan fired that gun.

The Grants had gone, quick as they came,
We heard the bushes rattle,
They disappeared into the night,
Like stolen highland cattle.

Where was Granny Claire ye ask,
Surely, she was there?
Hiding in the bushes, quiet
She does not easy scare.

We need yer Granny afterwards,
Not just to mend our britches.
If you've been wounded in a fight,
She's handy with the stitches.

****

The Laird is Embarrassed

Bring my plaid, let's go outside,
We should na' waste the sun.
We will na' get much more of it,
I'm glad hay makings done.

Will ye fetch ma glasses,
And someone fetch the book,
I canna remember all the tales,
I need to take a look.

I remember when I first came back.
We ran right out of flour,
The mill wheel was nae turning,
I could fix it in an hour!

So off I went up to the mill.
To try tae get it goin',
I took my Das' red flannel drawers.
To stop my arse from showing.

I was down there in the millpond,
When the Redcoats came a riding,
I was still a wanted man.
They could not catch me hiding.

But one of those wee soldiers,
His father was a miller.
He thought that he would fix the wheel.
My word that was a killer.

I was hiding neath the mill,
Hidden in the weed.
The cold was quietly freezing me,
The wheel must be freed,

I pulled and pushed and held my breath.
The mill wheel started turning,
I stayed under the water,
Though my lungs were burning.

I heard the redcoat's laughter,
And then I heard a pause
Hanging on the mill wheel
Were my Das' red flannel drawers.

When I climbed out the water,
The redcoats had long gone,
But I could na' hide the fact.
That I had nothing on.

Sitting in the sunshine,
spreading out their skirts
My wife and my good sister,
A hiding of my shirt.

Yer Grand Da looked a real sight,
My arse was turning blue.
My body white and shivering,
My face had gone red too.

I shouted they should turn their backs,
While I got out the water,
And hand me back my shirt and kilt,
And do it in short order.

Ach the pair of them just sat there,
Women at their worst,
Looking at my modesty,
And laughing fit to burst.

****

The Quid Pro Quo

The Duke agreed to help me,
We had to put him on the spot,
A petition for a pardon,
He'd really rather not.

Exposing his involvement,
With Black Jack did the trick,
Exposing his true loyalties,
The carrot and the stick,

Why is the Macdonald here?
With his tribe of sons,
The Duke must owe him money,
Here come the duelling guns!

So, he needs a second,
In a duel where no one dies.
They fire to miss each other.
Then honour is satisfied.

He demands his quid pro quo,
I must act as friend.
Make sure all is carried out,
All equal to the end,

The Duel was uneventful,
Honour was regained.
Mac Donald's sons were chirping,
Insults were exchanged.

The Duke took my petition,
I went home to my bride,
And asked her to put stitches,
In the sword wound in my side.

There was tight lipped silence,
with each stab of her needle
Her eyebrow raised in question,
When she hears me wheedle.

Aye, she can get a point across
Ye ken she is a witch,
And she's spelling displeasure.
rich in every stitch,

✳✳✳✳

A Visit from The Watch

Ye ken we welcome visitors,
That is the highland way,
Courtesy and politeness
When people come to stay

The Watch rode into Lallybroch,
As though they owned the place,
I think they were a bit surprised,
By the look upon my face.

They wanted food and lodging,
As promised them, by Jenny,
Like as not they'd eat a lot,
And then not pay a penny.

A pistol stuck right up my nose.
I'll not give them a meg,
We do not pay protection,
And I'm not about to beg.

Horrocks is a dead man,
A red coat, who deserted.
He for one will not be missed,
With the devil he has flirted.

I ken they've planned to rob the rents.
To carry out his plan
With Horrocks gone, they won't complain.
If I am now their man.

We ended up in Wentworth,
In shackles with the rest
This time for the gibbet.
Not the flogging post I guessed.

Mc Quarrie full of bluster,
With that rope around his neck,
He did not get a nice clean drop,
And I knew I was next.

I heard a shout for all to stop.
An order rattled through the air.
I was taken from the Gibbet.
And into Randall's Lair

✱✱✱✱

Black Jack Randall

Och how are you lot up sae late,
I'll tell one more, for you tae keep.
Dinna fash yer ma wi tears now,
Promise me, ye'll sleep.

Have yer sisters gone tae bed?
This one is for lads,
It's about old Black Jack Randall,
A man who's really bad.

I can nae tell it to the girls,
They'd be really scairt.
They'd be hiding in the closet,
Having real nightmares,

Black Jack was a Redcoat.
A Captain of Dragoon's,
Smart as paint, sat on his horse,
Commanding his platoons.

He liked to arrest highlanders.
Lock you in his jail.
The slightest thing - he'd flog you,
He liked to hear men wail.

Ye Ken the scars on Grand Da's back?
The ones which make ye stare – yes ye do!
They've been there for a long, long time,
Black Jack put them there.

Ye grand da was a brave man,
He wouldn't show his pain.
So, after he had been flogged once,
Jack flogged him once again.

Next time I was arrested,
I was rescued from my cell,
By Granny Claire and Murtagh.
I'll tell of him as well.

I remember lying on the floor,
When I heard, I don't know how,
Murtagh and my clansmen.
And the mooing of a cow.

Black Jack was in the passage,
Right behind the door,
When a rampant herd of highland coos.
Pinned him to the floor.

And so, they rescued Grand Da.
Not without a scandal
And we had some vengeance.
On that bastard Black Jack Randall.

****

The Bonnie Prince

Are ye sitting comfortable,
Time to listen in,
I'll tell ye of the Bonnie Prince,
I was friends with him.

He'll turn up in yer history,
That they teach at school,
I will tell ye something now,
That man was a fool.

He'd never run an army.
He had 'na been to war,
Had never been to Scotland,
What was he fighting for?

Twas all about the Scottish Crown
He wanted for his heid,
For that a lot of Scottish men,
Ended rather dead.

He liked to tell a story,
He talked a real good fight,
He also liked the ladies,
And staying out at night.

He thought that God would guide him,
That he was God's man on earth,
When most of us behind his back
Found him a thing of mirth.

Charles Edward Stuart,
For sure that was his name,
The rising up in 45
Was his claim to fame,

We tried hard to stop him.
Me and Granny Claire,
He would not see reason,
His God had sent him there.

They wrote a song about him,
You will know it aye!
About the lad born to be king,
Running away to Skye.

He wasn't such a bad man,
Just a bit miss led,
Now say yer own prayers children,
And get yerselves to bed.

✳✳✳✳

Parritch

When I was a wee small lad,
My mother passed away,
Her stone is in the graveyard,
I'll show it you one day.

My Da was grieving sorely,
Then Murtagh came to stay,
A godfather to protect me,
Until his dying day.

Murtagh taught me many things,
I didn't understand.
How to hunt and how to fish,
Living off the land,

When I was an outlaw,
Always on the run,
Murtagh Fitzgibbons Fraser,
Saw me as his son.

He was there at all the battles.
Taught our men to fight,
Taught simple farmers ways of war,
To fire a musket right.

He didn't much like Paris,
He thought it smelled of frogs,
Hated all the intrigue.
Thought them dirty dogs.

He was a dour and crusty man,
But a wicked sense of humour,
And he'd loved my mother,
If you believe the rumour.

In Versailles, in France ye ken,
We went to see the King.
To watch his Majesty, get dressed.
Was really quite a thing,

There he was his highness.
Looking like a twit.
Straining on the royal privy,
He could na have a sh**.

Jamie – they are children!
Try and keep it clean.
I've heard you tell this one before!
And your language gets obscene.

Mind yer whisht now woman,
There's no cause for alarm.
I will 'na tell them anything,
They'd not learn on a farm.

So, the King was on his toilet,
Trying tae have a poo.
He pushed and strained and sweated,
But nothing would come through.

Murtagh – he was quite surprised,
He made a verra rude suggestion.
For what his majesty should do.
To cure his bad digestion.

'Twas me – the Lord Brochtuarach.
Who gave the King the knowledge?
That he'd be regular as the clock
If he only ate his porridge.

Porridge is a peasant food,
Not a food for Kings,
But it keeps yer insides clear,
As well as other things.

After that the King of France
Took a shine to me.
The humble little Scottish oat,
Keeps yer bowels free!

There ye are – I kept it clean,
I'll no corrupt their minds,
I know what goes into their heids,
Comes out of their behinds.

A Brave but Warlike Man

Dougal was a warlike man,
My uncle so ye'll ken,
War chief of Mackenzie's,
He was a striking figure then.

The hero of the hour,
The stalemate Prestonpans,
He rode out on the marshland ,
So, we Scots could make our plans.

Mounted on his great grey horse,
He put aside his doubts,
120 yards the range,
There or thereabouts.

A brave man, and a lucky one,
He rode to test the ground,
If we could not cross that bog,
We'd have tae go around.

With the highland army cheering,
Aye - The Bonnie Prince was one.
He saw the British sniper.
Loading up his gun,

The man was good and accurate,
When he made the shot,
Dougal's hat flew off his heid,
He'd best get off the plot!

Now out of range, his swagger back,
He'd taunt the British Army,
A braver man I've never seen,
Though he was half barmy.

His finest hour, before his Prince
But before that day was done,
Dougal's bloodlust would appear,
And shame us, everyone.

He had no mercy for the wounded,
If they're British they must die,
And treating injured Redcoats!
He could not believe his eyes.

Screaming out our victory,
His killing rage not spent,
The Bonnie Prince will banish him,
From the battlefield ye Ken.

Branded a barbarian,
I've given him a role,
He's to recce out the British,
To find them is his goal.

He has his own dragoon of men.
Under his command,
Out of sight and out of mind,
The war chief has been damned.

****

I Wish I'd died

I'll tell ye of Culloden.
Yes - Yer Grand Da he was there,
I led the men from Lallybroch.
To that moor so cold and bare,

The fighting fierce
The highland charge, Into the British volley
Whoever gave that order,
Was surely versed in folly.

It makes me cold tae think of it,
I'm lying in the heather,
My eyes are crusted o'er with blood,
And the filthy Scottish weather,

Fallen, sprawled on top of me,
The body of a foe,
Breath rasping out between his lips,
His life about to go.

I hear the pleas of wounded men,
For help or maybe death,
A friend to look into their eyes,
As they take their last breath,

The Redcoats, with their bayonets.
No mercy, that is clear.
Steal our worthless little treasures,
That remind us why we're here.

Life is draining from me,
Black Jacks body has gone cold,
Nothing now to stop the end,
Hell calls me to its fold,

Oh, this is hell for certain,
They drag me from my grave.
Please let me lie here in this place,
My soul you cannot save.

But fate and time have other plans,
My death is not to be,
I'll be spending 20yrs in chains,
I made each one you see.

The shackles of the British,
May be most unkind,
But I've forged a lifetime of steel links,
The lock is in my mind.

I will exist, like marking time,
And what will be will be,
Is freedom really such a crime,
All mankind should live free.

The time will come, when two are one,
And the locks will open there,
There is one key to make me free,
The one I gave to Claire.

****

The Dun Bonnet

Have you seen Grand Da's glasses?
The ones I wear to read,
I hope ye have 'na sat on them,
I'd be verra sad indeed.

Sit down still ye braw we fiends,
Calm down ye swarm of gnats.
Pass my dram, it's story time.
I'll no tell tales tae brats.

Have ye heard the stories.
They tell of the Dun Bonnet.
A great tall man with red, red hair,
And the hat he kept upon it.

He had survived Culloden.
He came home bruised and battered.
His wife was dead – or gone away.
His family was shattered.

Not safe to live inside his home,
He found a hidden cave,
Hunted deer and squirrels,
The Scots folk thought him brave,

Redcoats came tae search for him,
All they found were ghosts,
He'd always get a warning,
From his local hosts.

His face on all the broadsheets,
His hair gave him away,
He had to keep it covered,
With a Bonnet so they say.

He stayed out on the run for years,
Living in a cave,
Providing for his family,
He'd not live as a slave.

But came a red coat Captain,
Sharper than the rest,
The Dun Bonnet was Red Jamie,
To surrender was the best.

I recall the day my sister,
That's yer granny Jenny,
Said she would 'na hand me in
For the English Penny.

Whole families were starving.
Turned out in the cold,
She'd feed a lot of bellies.
With the English gold.

So, I made her do a deal,
Yer Granny dobbed me in,
They took me off to Ardsmuir,
Kept me in chains ye ken.

All is for a reason,
At least that's what they say,
For at Ardsmuir Prison
I met with Lord John Grey.

Lord John and I became good friends,
Though he's English I confess,
He's very educated.
And he likes a game of chess.

We'd talk until the wee hours,
Then I'd go back to the cell,
And tell all of my clansmen,
Of the food we ate as well.

The men did not get fed a lot,
And some just loved to savour,
My description of those meals,
Imagine every flavour,

Talking of food, where's Granny Claire,
She late now with yer supper.
Ye'll all have indigestion,
I will nae see ya suffer.

Shall I read another?
From the pages in my book
Yer Granny's a great healer,
But she's no a verra good cook.

Maybe another story,
Will cure you of yer hunger,
Then go up quickly to yer beds,
Afore Granny keeps ye longer.

****

How Fergus lost his hand.

Gather round, sit by the fire,
Ay, don't upset the dog,
Poke the fire gently.
Put on another log,

Tonight, ye'll learn of Fergus,
I ken he is yer da.
I met him first in Paris,
I was there with your Grandma.

He wasn't known as Fergus then.
His real name Claudel,
He was living with the ladies,
At Madame Elise Hotel.

With the Bonnie Prince I was,
And some men who all were foreign.
I did'na a feel a single thing
When his hand went in my sporran.

Young Claudel was only nine.
Accomplished as a thief,
His ability to steal things.
Quite beyond belief,

When I found Sawney missing,
I searched all through our home,
Everybody looked for him,
But Sawney snake was gone.

My brother made that snake ye ken.
The year before he died.
It made me sad I'd lost it.
Yer grand da nearly cried.

Then I caught him thieving
I chased him down the street,
Turned him upside down and shook him.
My joy was then complete.

In amongst the other things
The handkerchiefs and money
Was my little wooden snake,
Claudel thought it was funny.

I took the little monkey home.
Called him Fergus by the by
Paid him then to steal for me,
Letters – like a spy.

When I was living in a cave,
The one there in the woods,
Redcoats came to look for me,
And to take our goods.

Fergus did a great brave thing,
He drew them off my scent,
By running round in circles
And shouting, in French ye ken

Corporal Macgregor was
The butt of this abuse.
And Young Fergus was too quick for him,
To chase him was no use.

Fergus was quick and nimble.
And wily as a Fox,
The soldiers were all weighed down.
With uniforms and stocks.

If he had na taunted them,
And run off as he planned,
He might have gotten clean away.
And kept his stealing hand.

I was hiding in the bushes.
When finally, he was caught.
And the Corporal cut his hand off,
He did it with his sword.

I could na fight the redcoats,
I was a wanted man,
My family would be hunted,
And our house burned down.

That's how yer Daddy Fergus.
Came to lose his hand,
Became a man of leisure.
He'd been the best thief in the land.

Now off to bed ye heathens,
Pick yerselves up off the floor.
Yer Grand da needs his beauty sleep,
He cannae think of more.

****

Prison Food

Don't tell me yer still hungry,
Ye only just had tea,
Ask yer granny if there's biscuits,
If there is- fetch some for me!

Hunger is an awful thing,
It gnaws inside yer guts,
If you're truly starving,
You really will eat rats.

Yes, yer Grand Da went to prison,
Treason was my crime,
Ardsmuir the establishment
Where I served my time.

I've survived on grass ye ken,
When I was on the run,
When there was no game to snare,
It was nae that much fun.

The men were always starving,
There was nae much to eat,
Porridge, and some bannocks,
But rarely any meat.

'Twas there I met with Lord John Grey,
Posted there as Governor,
He'd been sent there in disgrace.
It's a posting without honour.

And I was the leader,
The spokesman for the men,
MacDuh is what they called me.
In Ardsmuir – ye ken

His Lordship liked a game of chess,
To occupy his mind,
He needed an opponent,
I'm the only one he'd find.

I'd get to go for dinner,
Maybe once a week,
A chance to fill my belly,
With good food so to speak.

Pheasant in a red wine sauce,
With mashed neeps and tatties
And afterwards a glass of port,
While the men were eating ratties!

A game of chess sat by his fire,
Some educated chat,
Discussion on the needs of ours,
In the cells and that.

When I went back to the cell
I'd tell stories of my night,
Slowly, recount everything,
Aye - I'd have tae get it right.

I'd tell them the ingredients,
What went in the pot?
The smell, the taste, the texture,
Where the bird was shot.

The richness of the red wine sauce,
The juicy taste of meat,
The way it dribbled down my throat,
Their rapture was complete.

For men who hadn't eaten,
The tale was full of flavour.
I'd tell the best bits over.
Every mouthful they would savour.

✳✳✳✳

Helwater

Are you sitting waiting,
Sorry for delay,
I'm thinking of the place I went,
Paroled by Lord John Grey

Arriving at Helwater
Indentured as a groom.
To serve the Lord Dunsany
At least there's loads of room.

His Lordship was a fair man.
He treats his staff alright.
But his wife Lady Dunsany
Hated Jacobites.

Not known by my proper name
Its best I'm known as Mac.
It's better here than Ardsmuir.
With sunshine on my back

His Lordship has two daughters.
The eldest one Geneva
Spoiled, petulant and headstrong.
She's a schemer and deceiver.

Betrothed to the Earl of Ellesmere
Who's older than her father.
She demands I take her off to bed.
Because it's me she'd rather.

She threatened me with prison.
She threatened all my kin.
She'll tell her mother I'm Red Jamie
God knows what she'd make of him.

So, I climb in through the window.
And creep along the halls
For just the one night only
She's got me by the balls.

She visits some months later.
I hand her off the carriage.
She's clearly been up the duff.
Since early in her marriage.

Jamie! spare the graphic details,
They don't need that much knowledge,
I'm sure they'll learn the facts of life,
When they go to college.

A boy is born, his mother dies.
The Earl calls him a bastard.
He calls his teenage wife a whore.
Her bed he hadn't mastered.

~ 67 ~

He threatens then to kill the boy.
I'm called to stop the trouble.
I end up shooting the old Earl.
The child could be my double.

It's all hushed up and swept away.
Under an English rug
Misadventure says the coroner.
And dismisses with a shrug.

Six years on I'm pardoned.
Released to return home.
Leaving Young Lord Ellesmere
Despite how fond I've grown.

One day he'll see a likeness.
In the mirror looking back
And realise his father.
Is a Scottish groom called Mac?

****

A Verra English Uncle

Sit still ye braw wee heathens,
Before ye trash the house,
Creep ye softly down the hall,
Quiet as a mouse.

Did ye see the panel,
Ripped from side to side,
The Redcoats did that one fine day,
When I'd come tae hide.

We left it thus, so all can see.
The carnage caused by conflict,
The mindless acts of damage caused,
When looking for a convict.

Not all English men are bad,
A few have saved my life,
And yer Granny Claire's a Sassenach,
Yes, I have an English wife.

And you have an uncle,
You may find him in a book,
He is 9th Earl of Ellesmere,
You may want to take a look.

He may never come tae Scotland,
He does na own his roots,
He is my son, and just like his da,
Gets too big for his boots.

If ye should ever meet him,
Just look in the mirror,
His likeness to yer ma – and me,
Just might make ye shiver.

Raised to be a gentleman,
A wealthy English Earl,
It's better that he stays away,
From the Pipers Skirl,

But I'd give my mortal soul,
Yer Gran Da's not a liar,
To see my Willies English boots,
Stood by my Scottish fire.

Come Sassenach, join us here,
Come out of yer lair,
Pour a dram and raise a glass,
To a verra English heir.

✳✳✳✳

St Anthony of lost things

He had the best of everything,
He grew up, loud and spoiled,
Not allowed to play outside,
Lest his clothes got soiled,

Escape was in the stables,
The time he spent with horses,
He learned to ride, and care for them,
And the pull of other forces,

All the grooms were kind to him,
But I was the one called Mac,
The one who taught him everything,
I remember looking back.

He used to sneak up to my loft,
I lived there with the hay,
He'd catch me at remembering.
In my papist way,

I told him of St Anthony,
While I lit a flame,
And prayed for all my lost ones,
Each one I would name,

My sister, and My brother, called Willie.
Just like he,
My mother and my godfather,
My Scottish family!

Then he saw a grown man cry,
The first time in his life,
When I prayed that St Anthony
Would not forget my wife.

He wants to be a papist,
He wants to be like Mac,
So, I baptised him, James like me!
I remember looking back.

My thumb upon his forehead,
The father and the son,
And He'd never tell his granny,
What he had become.

✳✳✳✳

The Printer

When I returned from Helwater,
My life was in a mess.
I did some things I now regret,
That I will confess.

A day like any other day,
A respectable façade,
A cover for my murky trade
To make detection hard.

The web I wove around myself.
To hold it all together,
was born of lies and of deceit.
It wouldn't stand much more weather.

I'd tried to live the settled life.
I'd tried to love another,
Her children are my family,
But I couldn't stand the mother.

So, I open up the print shop.
And settle to my work.
Pen has more power now than sword.
Print more power than dirk.

Thought nothing of the chiming door.
Thought Geordie was returning.
Chided him for taking time.
My irritation burning.

A voice not heard for twenty years.
But still a clear as bells
Spoke from above and put my thoughts.
In seven kinds of hells.

That voice embodied in a face.
And a form not an illusion
Threw my fragile web of lies.
Into a mass confusion.

For twenty years I had not slept
Without thought of her returning
For twenty years I kept alive.
Her memory, and the yearning.

And here she is, a real thing.
Not seen through a fever
A living, breathing, solid Claire.
Who I have loved forever?

I felt the blood drain from my face,
My legs like went weak for sure.
The ale pot fell before me,
And beat me to the floor.

How would I start to tell her?
Of the mess that is my life
That in the time she was away.
Laoghaire became my wife.

Claire is all for honesty.
But I knew that I must lie.
I need just to keep her there.
And pray she did not fly.

I would tell her bit by bit.
Of most that I had done
The tangle which was now my life
And prayed she would not run.

***

Silkie Island

Have ye heard of Silkies,
I think ye call them seals.
They live on an island,
And eat fish for all their meals

That island is na far from here,
Ye can see it from the shore,
I ken the day I swam there,
When I escaped Ardsmuir.

The water was so cold ye ken.
My flesh was turning blue,
The current like to pull me down,
But I knew I'd get through.

'Twas then I saw the silkie.
Black and gleaming like the night,
Eyes that stared into your soul
It gave me quite a fright.

They called my da a silkie,
For his hair of black,
But that's another story.
Let's get back on track.

The silkies breath was rank with fish.
I felt it land on me.
Then he slipped into the water
And glided out to sea.

It's a verra rocky island.
There's an old Kirk on the cliff,
Ruined now and empty.
The climb up there is stiff.

'Twas said that there was treasure,
Hidden in the kirk,
Guarded by a white witch,
But surely worth the work.

I thought it was yer Granny Claire,
Travelled back in time,
Come again to set me free.
That would be worth the climb.

I shouted loud to find my Claire,
But she was truly gone,
Hiding in the mist of time,
More of her – anon.

I found the box of treasure,
Hidden in the wall,
I took from it one sapphire,
Yes, really that was all.

I hid that box for time to come,
I marked its value well,
But the guardian of this treasure,
Was one step away from hell.

I swam back through the current,
My wife was truly gone,
And the sapphire I had taken.
Well, I gave it to Lord John.

Now off to bed wee rascals,
Dream dreams of all that's good,
Grand da will have another dram,
If yer granny'd thinks I could.

****

A long Sea Voyage.

We've travelled far across the sea,
Me and yer granny Claire,
Ye'll ken she's said how sick I get,
Just smelling salty air.

We had a big adventure,
Finding yer cousin Ian
Yes – the one who is a Mohawk Brave,
Sit down ye cheeky we'an.

On a ship the Artemis,
Owned by my cousin Jared,
Yes – the one who sold the wine,
The one who lived in Paris.

Settle down now, listen,
Or I'll pack ye off to bed.
If ye keep on interruptin.
List to what I've said.

The Artemis a sturdy ship,
Powered then by sails,
Her crew were superstitious ay,
So, we touched the horseshoe nails.

Then the wind ceased blowing,
She stopped – we were becalmed.
Running out of water,
I feared we would be harmed.

Wily Mr Willoughby,
Chinese – have I told.
I found him sleeping on the dock.
In Scotland in the cold.

Yi Tien Cho – his real name,
Leans against heaven.
A courtier from the Chinese court.
Skilled in Chinese medicine.

He cured me of the seasickness.
With needles long and fine
Stuck at places in my heid.
Just like a porcupine!

He had been writing poems,
A story of his life,
He threw them all over the side,
The wind came back to life,

This satisfied the sailors,
And it was not to be,
They shelved a plan, to throw a man.
For luck, into the sea.

Wily little Willoughby
Watched the birds aloft.
When they fly low to the water,
A breath of wind will waft.

When the birds are flying high,
The upper air is calm.
No wind about to fill the sails.
The sailors need a charm.

Rain came down to fill the kegs.
We had our fill of water.
And set off for Jamaica,
With more sail than we ought ter.

Next, I'll tell of Granny Claire.
She had adventures too.
As Doctor on a 74.
Healing all the crew.

I can see ye sleeping,
Go quietly to yer beds.
Crawl under yer covers
And rest ye weary heads.

A Verra Good Distraction.

The Theatre in Wilmington,
Is where we can be found,
A night out in society,
Opportunities abound,

Well, ye know I've read the classics,
They are not strange to me,
But the play they are enacting,
Is not my cup of tea.

And Tryon has informed me.
That he sent his men
To trap the regulators,
That's Murtagh's gang ye ken.

I really need to warn him,
But I'm stuck in here,
I need a big distraction,
Make sure the coast is clear.

Good fortune has me seated,
Next to Edmond Fanning,
So, I poke him in his hernia,
That didn't take much planning.

Fanning needs a doctor quick,
Or he's like to die.
Claire's will need her scalpels.
I went, quickly I won't lie.

Hitched a ride with Washington.
My Alibi now in place
Sent Fergus to tell Murtagh,
Not to show his face.

Back to the Theatre,
Claire still in her gown,
Tryon and some big strong men,
Holding Fanning down.

His physician turns up to the show,
Or should we say this farce,
To cure Fanning's hernia,
Puff smoke up his arse,

But Granny has her scalpel out,
And is sticking to her cause,
She fixes Fanning's hernia.
To tumultuous applause.

Murtagh has escaped again,
And here's the funny thing.
Tryon was so distracted,
He did not suspect a thing.

I'd better have another dram,
Do not hear me wrong.
You lot better go to bed.
Morning won't be long.

Yer Granny, she will scold me.
You'll all be late for school,
She'll tak her scalpel to my bits
If yer don't obey her rules.

✳✳✳✳

Grand Da and the Bear.

Where's my old plaid Sassenach,
I hope ye have nae thrown it,
I've only worn it thirty years,
If there's holes, you could'a sewn it.

Ah there it is, now let's sit down.
Get comfy in my chair,
I'll tell you of the very night,
I fought and killed a bear.

'Twas before we had the land ye ken.
Just me and Granny Claire,
Travelled through the mountains,
Looked for a home to share.

We found a place to spend the night,
Camping by a stream,
I was cooking fish we'd caught.
When I heard her scream.

It came out of the bushes,
Its beady eyes were gleaming,
Its claws were long as short swords.
Foam from its mouth was streaming,

I dropped the fish; I grabbed my knife.
And as swiftly as I dare.
I pushed your granny out the way,
And wrestled with the bear.

The thick black fur was fit to choke,
I stank of something foul,
It's claws it sank into my back,
It really made me howl.

I'd never fought a beast this strong,
Armed only with a knife,
If I couldn't kill it verra soon,
The bear would end my life.

I stabbed and slashed,
It tried to bite; its breath was in my ear.
It pinned me down, the world went black,
My time was up I fear,

I felt my knife pierce through its hide,
I heard the rip of skin,
I smelled the blood, and stink of guts,
I think I might just win,

I pushed myself up to my feet,
I prayed and made a wish,
And then yer very helpful granny
Hit me with the fish.

Are ye listening Sassenach,
You've an arm tae swing a trout.
A fish is not a weapon.
But you fair near knocked me out!

****

Rescuing Roger

Sassenach are ye out there,
Come sit and make me smile,
We have na drunk a dram or two.
Together for a while.

Do ye remember Frasers Ridge.
Before the land was tamed
When Roger came to look for Bree,
I still feel quite ashamed.

We knew nought of Bonnet,
And her trying to buy your ring,
Only that she'd been attacked,
Well, raped – and that did sting.

No one knew the whole of it,
I didn't know the truth.
And Lizzie acted for the best,
Accounting for her youth,

Angry does nae cover it,
My temper was a villain.
And when I came across the man,
'Twas in my mind to kill him.

I dinna need a weapon,
I've one with either fist
I did'na wait for answers,
Lost in a red mist.

Half alive and sold as slave.
A spring lamb to the slaughter,
When at last the truth came out,
I nearly lost my daughter.

And so, began the long trek north,
To track the Indian traders,
To bargain for our Roger Mac,
Not get mistook for raiders.

The Mohawk are not stupid,
They know the worth of men,
They adopt some folk into their tribe,
The useful ones ye ken.

The stone you carried angered them,
It came from one who travelled,
Who tried to warn of white man's ways,
Their life to be unravelled.

Roger would replace a brave,
He had survived the walk.
Hundreds of miles, behind a horse.
He could hardly talk.

I'd ha stayed there Sassenach,
To heal things with my daughter,
I did'na ken what Ian said,
When he made the deal for Roger.

He'd learned the Indian customs,
Myers had filled his heid.
And now he was to stay with them,
Ach, his mother' d see me dead.

But Ian is the man he is,
Because he made that break,
Buckskins and a tomahawk,
A man of honour makes,

Roger came back to the fold,
And I was soon forgiven,
Then Ian and his dog returned,
Life was again worth living.

Do ye think the weans now,
Will come to understand,
They need to see the whole of things.
Before they raise a hand.

Their Grand Da, was impulsive,
Some will say still is,
Acting without thinking,
Is a trait of his?

What do you think Sassenach?
Will they get it right?
Pick their battles carefully,
And know which ones to fight.

I need tae take ye Sassenach,
We're a bit old fer the floor,
Let me take ye up to bed.
And maybe bolt the door!

****

Hunting Bees

Ye ken I did'na meet yer ma.
And who she'd grown to be,
Yer Granny left her in her time,
'Twas safer there, ye see.

She came to warn us through the stones.
Of something that she'd found,
The house we'd built on Frasers Ridge,
Would burn down to the ground.

The paper said, we both were dead,
Yer Granny Claire and me,
You couldn't read the printed date.
When 'twas supposed to be.

I had to get to know her,
So, we went hunting bees,
Find out more about her,
Underneath the trees.

When your hunting bees ye ken,
First you find their flowers,
Ye follow them, through the woods,
Keep watch on them for hours.

Quietly you find the tree,
Where they made their home,
Ye see they all live in one place,
And then go out to roam.

When you find their hiding place.
You wait until it's dark,
For that's when all the bees are home.
And you can find yer mark.

Puff a bit o' smoke in,
Makes them go tae sleep.
Then you put them in yer bag,
The whole swarm ye keep.

When they wake in the morning,
They are in a different place,
And you have honey for yer bread,
Or smeared across yer face.

Yer mother's good at hunting,
She's a crack shot too ye see,
Ye dinnae mess with yer mother,
The disturbance we call Bree.

It's late now, ye'll be getting cold.
Best you get off up to bed,
Dream of honey, on yer toast
Or upon yer bread.

Go quietly, ma will tuck you in.
No - I'm not making a joke,
If you lot don't go off to sleep,
I'll be up there puffing smoke!

****

Brownsville

I think I need a second dram,
To tell the Brownsville tale
Of my Captain Roger Mac,
And a venture doomed to fail.

Now Brownsville is a funny place,
It's verra, verra strange,
All the folk are family,
Ye ken they're no quite sane.

Forming a militia,
I needed fighting men,
There's lots of them in Brownsville,
They're a violent lot, ye ken.

Sent off on an errand.
I sent in Roger Mac,
To recruit the Browns to fight with us,
He went off down the track.

The reception wasn't pleasant,
Lionel Brown would not give quarter,
To Isiah Morton
Who had defiled his daughter?

A thorny problem to be solved,
Lionel has but one,
To cut off our Isiah's balls,
Then shoot him with his gun.

When Claire and I rode into town
The men had all been drinking,
Pissed as crickets most of them,
What was Roger thinking.

And Roger Mac my Captain
Deep amongst this throng,
Doing what he does the best,
Giving them a song.

I was nae really all that pleased,
They'd used up all the Whisky.
The Browns were still not happy,
The atmosphere was risky.

Roger had but one plan.
And he did confess,
He got them drunk and waited,
For me to sort this mess.

Ay Rogers not a fighter,
Recruiting's not his game
But when it comes to singing songs.
He puts us all to shame.

****

A Coat of Red

Have you got yer nightclothes on?
Has the baby got her rattle?
Sit down now and listen hard.
We're going into battle.

A sly man governor Tryon,
As wily as a Scot,
Always tries to get his way,
And does as like as not.

I'd raised a good militia,
And brought them to the fray,
To fight the regulators
At Alamance that day.

He knew what he was doing,
I'd rather I was dead,
Than turn out on a battlefield
In a coat of red.

He'd even got my measurements.
It was a perfect fit.
But it burned me when I put it on,
I canna get out of it.

He knows that as a Scotsman,
I won't be for the King,
To dress me in a coat of red
Is a power thing.

Designed to show the dominance.
Of England and the Crown
Humiliate our spirit,
Completely grind us down.

If I wear this coat of red
I'll stand out in the crowd,
It puts a target on my back.
Says 'shoot me' right out loud.

I'm no a verra vain man.
But as I said tae Claire,
Red is nae my colour,
It clashes with ma hair.

When the fight was over,
The regulators beat,
I ripped off that blood red jacket,
And threw it at his feet.

Children I was sad that day,
Enough tae make me cry,
One of my men shot Murtagh.
I saw my godfather die,

Fill my glass, I'll drink a toast.
And pour one for yer Gran.
We'll drink a toast to Murtagh!
Exasperating man

✳✳✳✳

The Plague of Locusts

Here's one I have nae told ye,
It's all about yer da,
Wee Roger Mac – a clever man,
And my daughter - she's yer ma!

Me and Granny were away,
Roger was in charge,
Folk would likely go to him.
With problems, small and large.

There was a buzzing in the air,
And no – it wasn't bees!
A swarm of locusts filled the sky,
Covering the trees,

This evil little beastie
Eats with all its might,
Will ruin all your growing crops.
Right before your sight,

What could they do on Frasers Ridge,
Rogers does not farm
But his educated thinking
Saved the ridge from harm.

To stop a swarm of insects,
Create a cloud of smoke,
Most of them will fly on by,
If they land, they'll choke.

He lined the fields with pots of shite.
Mixed it up with earth.
It burned with a disgusting smell,
And smoked for all it's worth.

I would na have known just what tae do.
But Roger earned his pay.
Creating smoke – stopped our folk,
Losing all they had that day.

Roger Mac is a professor,
But not what you expect,
The man who wed my daughter.
Had now earned my respect.

****

Snake Bite

A very gruesome story
I'm about to tell.
So, huddle close together.
Listen to it well.

Once I was out hunting
And made a big mistake.
Fixated on the buffalo.
I didn't see the snake.

Me and good old Roger Mac,
We're hiding by a tree.
The bastard sunk its fangs in.
Just above my knee.

(That's the snake not Roger ye ken)

The snake was verra venomous.
I began to fail,
I thought that I might die right there.
Lying on the trail.

Roger kept me going,
Good old Roger Mac,
Tied me to a homemade sledge,
And then he dragged me back.

He prayed for me in English,
The Presbyterian twit,
I like my prayers in Latin,
And there's an end to it.

Granny Claire was sore afraid,
Thinking I would pass,
The Browns had broken her syringe.
She could'na jab my arse.

She packed the wound with maggots.
Wriggly little critters,
They eat the dead infected flesh,
They quite gave me the jitters.

Grand da was in a right bad way,
I could na take much more,
But I had to take some action,
When yer granny fetched her saw.

She would take my leg off.
To cut off the infection,
I'd rather die with both my legs.
Was my sad reflection.

I staggered to our bedroom,
I put myself tae bed,
I waited for yer granny Claire.
To come and soothe my heid.

Yer Ma came to my rescue,
My Bree made a syringe,
She used the fangs from that old snake.
To put Claire's medicine in.

It was rather painful,
She jabbed me in the wound.
Rather than in my arse,
I yelped like a hound.

Yer Grannies penicillin,
Killed off the infection,
Ye know she is my heart and soul.
And also, my protection.

She's mended me a lot more times,
Then the sky has stars,
If ye like, and yer verra good,
I'll show ye all the scars!

✳✳✳✳

My Buffalo Gals

Shut the door, keep out the draught,
Ach, yer granny's in the kitchen,
I'm reminded of another tale,
Ye ken my leg is itchin.

I was lying in my bed,
Recoverin from the snake,
I was sweatin with a fever,
All my bones did ache,

I could see the laundry drying,
Hanging on the line,
Blowing in the autumn breeze,
The weather was quite fine,

Lizzie getting on with chores,
Jemmy by her side,
Ah my first wee grandson,
He fills me up wi pride!

I did'na see what happened next,
But I heard them scream,
Brianna running 'cross the grass.
Was this some form of dream,

A massive, woolly buffalo,
With horns, and eyes of red,
Was eyeing up Young Jemmy,
If it charged, he would be dead.

It pawed the ground and snorted,
It eyed the flapping sheet.
It heard poor Lizzie screaming,
Her terror was complete.

Ah Bree, my Bonnie, fearless lass.
The instincts of a mother,
'Twas, brave the thing ye did that day,
Ye truly are my daughter,

Waving at that massive beast,
Ye face with anger filled.
I saw it throw ye in the air,
I feared ye might be killed,

I dragged myself to action,
I fell out through the door,
Naked save a blanket,
I needn't have I'm sure.

I heard yer granny shouting,
I heard the rifles CRACK.
I saw the great beast falling,
And Bree bouncing off it's back.

I can trust my women folk,
They both can fire a rifle,
Both are pretty accurate,
With them ye do not trifle.

And I endured the wrath of Claire,
For straying from my bed,
She called me all the stupid things,
She thought of in her head.

A job now for the butcher,
There's half a ton of meat,
We wouldn't starve this winter,
We've plenty now tae eat.

I'm sure granny left some maggots,
If I may say so bold
My leg it itches like a fiend,
When the weathers cold.

That's how they killed the buffalo.
And I'm saying this in fun.
Don't mess with yer granny.
She's a danger with a gun!

****

Nine Lives

I was told once that I have nine lives,
That nine times I would die,
Sometimes I try and count them up,
God knows why I try,

One – was when they flogged me,
The day my father died,
Two – the axe wound in my heid,
About which Dougal lied.

Three – was tortured by Black Jack,
When You brought me from the dark,
Four was on Culloden field,
Where I should have left my mark.

Five- was shot by Laoghaire, when You
Came back as my wife.
Six – a snake bite to my leg
fever nearly took That life.

If I count the shipwreck
Then I'm up to seven,
And all the times I'm shot and stabbed.
That makes about eleven.

Sassenach, I'd value
Your professional opinion,
Which bits of me are still alive,
They're all in your dominion.

Come check out all my faculties,
I think there's still some life,
Take inventory of all my parts.
It's your duty as my wife!

＊＊＊＊

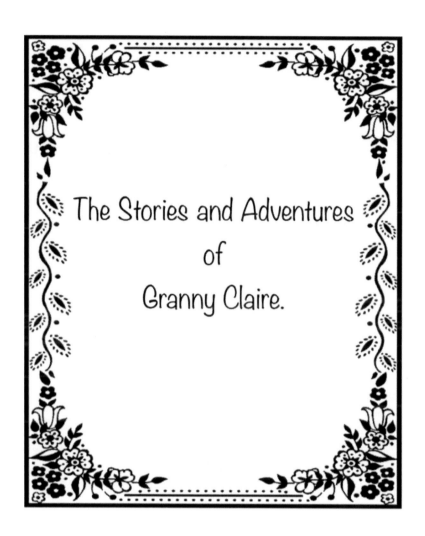

The Stories and Adventures of Granny Claire.

Listening in the Kitchen

I'm out in the kitchen,
He thinks I've no idea.
When he is telling stories
What those kids may hear,

He loves to tell his stories.
Sit back and reminisce,
But some are not exactly,
A gentle bedtime kiss.

He tells them so completely.
In the language of the day,
He forgets that in this time of ours,
Our grandkids will not stay.

They will all go home you see,
And no one else can know.
That they visit Grand da,
200 years ago.

His language is emotive,
He has a way with words,
If a bit old fashioned,
We no longer talk of turds.

But they are learning of their family.
And how it once was riven.
And if they learn to swear in Gaelic.
Grand da, will not be forgiven.

And when it comes to cooking
I admit - I'd rather not.
If he chooses not to eat it,
I could hit him with the pot.

****

Falling Through Time

The flowers were forget me nots.
I knelt to pick a few,
To add to my collection,
Their pretty shade of blue.

A clump of hardy flowers,
Nestled at its base,
The massive granite standing stone,
Inches from my face,

A humming noise, A sound like screams
The crashing guns of battle
The feel of a magnetic pull,
My senses start to rattle,

I can't resist the fatal pull,
The largest stone of all,
Tempts me now to touch it,
I must obey its call.

I place my hand upon it,
The world at once is black,
The acrid smell of ozone
My body starts to crack,

I feel like I am torn apart,
Almost vapourised,
My bones are disassembled,
Then rematerialized.

It's a feeling like no other,
Like dropping in a lift
A crazy rollercoaster,
Or falling off a cliff,

The light is truly blinding,
Fit to mesmerise,
A hundred thousand lightbulbs
All shining in your eyes,

You hear the noises of creation.
And the screaming of the dead,
A hundred new sensations
Exploding in your head,

And all this happens in a flash,
It's chaos without limit.
Falling through the veil of time,
Only takes a minute.

****

Boar Hunt

A hairy pig, with razor tusks,
Sharp enough to kill,
Not for the faint hearted.
To hunt a boar takes skill.

A tradition at the gathering,
The Clansmen's form of fun
A tinchel in the woodland scrub,
Wild Boar on the run,

Curly hair, a mass of black,
Eyes, tiny, red, and gleaming,
Deceptive in its size and speed,
Steam from its nostrils streaming.

Poor Geordie gored, right through his leg,
If I can stop this bleeding,
I cannot mend his ruptured guts.
His life is now receding,

A different side of Dougal,
He will not leave his friend,
He talks to him of better times,
Comfort to the end.

He's worked out I've seen men die,
But will not know the place.
I gave comfort to the wounded,
Stitched up the human race,

Now Geordies back upon his farm,
Walking on the heather,
Will I go back to my home too?
Or be lost in time forever?

****

Breakfast Scottish Style

Just to set the scene a bit
I shall start the night before.
Grand Da spent a cold hard night.
Asleep outside my door.

The Inn was full of drunkards.
And with my safety on his mind
He feared I might have 'visitors.
Of a most unwelcome kind.

At breakfast in the morning
I was sat amongst the men.
Porridge doled out for breakfast.
But an atmosphere – ye ken

I don't have much Gaelic.
Their signals were quite clear.
The rabble making phallic signs.
And grinning ear to ear.

Angus slammed his bowl down.
Then picked up his dirk,
Rupert drew his breath in.
Murtagh gave a smirk.

Even Ned began to look around.
For a convenient place to hide
And Dougal quietly nodded.
At Willie by my side.

Angus growled and strolled across
Said something to the lad.
Rammed his head into his porridge.
Called him something really bad.

Bodies crashing everywhere.
Plates and fists were thrown.
I sat in the corner.
Puzzled and alone.

Bloody Scots must they pick.
A fight at any chance
More bodies thrown against the wall.
A stamping, kicking dance.

It ended quick as it began.
The losers having fled.
I patched up Mackenzie wounds.
Bandaged Mackenzie heads.

As guest of the Mackenzie,
They may insult me to be sure.
But god help any other man.
Who calls their guest a whore!

I suppose I must be thankful.
That the finest of all forces
My red haired, protector
Had been sent to feed the horses.

****

I didn't want to stay.

Here's a story of my own,
Of how I came to tarry
When I really didn't mean to stay,
Let alone to marry.

I was washing in the stream.
taken unawares,
And here comes lieutenant Foster
to complicate affairs.

I was a guest of the Mackenzie,
Dougal gave advice.
My reply was not convincing,
The Lieutenant asked me twice.

Just to make quite sure of me,
We are to go with him,
To the Garrison Commander
Who is stationed at some Inn.

I thought it would be safer,
But I was quite naïve,
If I thought the British Army,
Would all my lies believe.

We are taken to an upper room,
Where an English Brigadier,
Is dining with his colleagues,
On the best of Scottish deer.

He tries humiliating Dougal,
With a denigrating show,
How the War Chief kept his temper
I really do not know.

This simpering, foppish, idiot,
Is believing all my lies,
I may just get away with this,
Oh, what a surprise.

Then In storms Black Jack Randall
It does not give him cheer.
To find War Chief Mackenzie
In the Tap Room drinking beer.

I am given to Jack Randall.
And I must impress,
The Brigadier told him.
I'm to go to Inverness.

But Jack has ideas of his own,
He can't believe his eyes.
I've fallen right into his trap,
He believes me a spy.

A plausible, but cruel man,
He gets his kicks from violence,
Another punch, another kick,
I may just break my silence.

Dougal called an end to it,
Came to a decision.
This treatment on Mackenzie land.
Was a great imposition.

But the price I had to pay,
Was to be there at the Fort,
Submit to further questions,
Or be hunted without thought.

A game of chess, played with my life,
You cannot compel a Scot,
Be questioned by the British,
If they'd rather not.

If I am to win this game,
As a widow, I must wed,
And become a Scottish wife,
And he must take me to bed.

So, in one day it was arranged,
That I would wed young Jamie,
It could have been Rupert,
But they'd have had to pay me!

So that's why I wed your Grand da,
It wasn't loves young dream,
And in his darker moments,
He says he 'took one for the team'.

****

Idle Hands

Just before the rising.
We spent some time in France.
Trying to subvert the cause,
The Jacobite advance

An endless round of pointlessness
Of gossip and taking tea,
Is this all I can look forward to,
Here in gay Paree!

These vapid Parisienne women
Are really not my scene.
Especially when I'm turning.
Morning sickness green.

I feel like I'm abandoned,
With just this house to run,
Sitting in my gilded cage,
While he has all the fun!

He won't be very happy,
But I'm going to volunteer,
As a healer in the Hospital,
Now that's a good idea.

Your Grand Da stayed out late at night.
Talking politics and treason
At least I'll occupy my day.
And give my life a reason.

Working late and going home
With tales of suppurations
Stitching wounds, and bandaging
And nasty amputations.

Well, it went down like a lead balloon,
It nearly wrecked our marriage,
Should have listened to what Murtagh said,
When we got into the carriage.

✳✳✳✳

Mother Hildegarde

A god daughter of royalty,
She is the driving force and more.
At The hospital of Angels
Where they treat the poor.

Saintly mother Hildegarde,
Is older than the hills,
Her life devout to serve her god,
With medicine and pills.

She glides amongst the patients,
Creates calm all round.
And with her little dog Bouton,
Sniff's infection, in a wound.

Educated, musical.
She has no time for fools,
Believes in talking honestly,
Does not like breaking rules.

When Faith was born, she told a lie.
That she lived at birth,
You may not name a baby,
Born dead, for all your worth

A secret kept by her and Claire.
She shook her head and frowned,
Named her Faith, and buried her,
In consecrated ground.

****

An Audience

Why?
a year was all I asked for,
I was carrying our child,
You stupid, idiotic man,
Why must you be so wild.

You Promised!
You swore you wouldn't do it,
You said there'd be no dual
But then you did it anyway,
You treat me like a fool.

Blood
I lost our precious baby,
I can do no more,
The life we made between us,
Is blood upon the floor

Death
I nearly died, I should have,
Raymond saved my life,
And you – locked in the Bastille,
As if you have no wife.

Begging
Yet again I'm begging.
This time to a King,
To get you out of prison,
There's bound to be a sting,

Friends
Dearest mother Hildegarde
Warned me what the debt would be.
Will you forgive what I must do,
To make him set you free.

The King
Got up in my finest gown,
An audience with the King,
He has more in store for me,
Than his customary thing!

Witchcraft
He makes me judge and jury,
Raymond and St Germaine,
Who is black and who is white?
One of them is damned.

Sleight of hand.
I did not see him do it,
Put the poison in the cup,
St Germain had no great choice.
But to drink it up.

Black
He knew that it was deadly.
My pendant had turned black.
A warning of the poison,
But there was no turning back.

Banished
Banished then from all of France.
Master Raymond has his life,
He'll turn up in another time,
Maybe with less strife.

Humiliated,
And I was forced to bed the King,
To pay for your frustration
A pure act of dominance.
One last humiliation.

Forgiven.
I know now about Fergus,
And I know I can forgive,
But take me home to Scotland,
Let's find a place to live.

Free
I'm done with all the spying.
The intrigue and the lies,
Dirty deceitful Paris,
A city where Faith dies.

Unravelling in Boston

I promised that I would go back,
Grand Da sent me through the stones,
I'd have given all to stay with him,
I loved him to his bones.

A woman looking like a tramp,
Stumbled down the road,
Outlandish clothes from bygone days,
Distressed, and lost and cold.

I must have been a frightening sight,
To anyone who saw
This starving, feral, unkempt thing,
Who'd travelled from that moor.

They tried to tell me I was mad,
I had no explanation,
Well, none they could believe at least.
It adds to my frustration.

My need to know of history,
The fate of all the Clans,
Of Stirling and Culloden
And of Preston pans.

And Frank my previous husband – he thought I was
lying
That I ran off with a lad,
That patronising bastard,
Believed I had gone mad.

He would not stay in Scotland,
He couldn't abide the chatter,
He took a job in Boston,
My views did not matter,

Dress to please your husband,
Look pretty for the boss,
These 1950s standards,
Had me at a loss,

Patronised, redundant,
This role was badly cast,
At least the men respected me,
In my Scottish Highland past.

I was not cut out to be.
Just a housewife and a mother,
A domesticated dolly,
Trained to serve another.

From one domestic crisis,
To another meal disaster,
The veneer was really wearing thin,
Frank was not my master.

At night, my thoughts went wandering,
And every time would find,
A memory of some part of him
His body and his mind.

And I have a living memory,
I carried her with me,
Will she ever know her father?
Will he ever know Bree?

I tried hard to move on from there,
It became a pantomime,
Forget about your Grand Da!
There was never enough time.

✳✳✳✳

Return Visit

I swore I'd not set foot here,
I'd been here once before,
And now I stared across the place,
They call Drummossie moor.

That day with Frank I could not know,
This place so soaked in blood.
Would take from me a lifetime,
Condemn me where I stood,

So here I am, to say goodbye,
To tie up my loose ends,
Not just to you, Soldier,
I say goodbye to friends.

The Fraser Stone, is this the place?
Do you lie beneath?
Buried with your kinsmen,
In the ground below my feet.

I'll tell you of our daughter,
Before I say goodbye,
She really is so much like you,
And I really must not cry.

Our wedding gift, your good luck charm.
Displayed beneath the glass,
Did it mark the place you fell?
Was it in this very grass?

And then I went and saw the house,
The dooryard overgrown,
The windows smashed or boarded up,
For Sale – who could have known.

What drew me back to Scotland?
Was it really a goodbye?
I cannot forget you,
No matter how I try.

I tried before, I tried with Frank.
To forget you is my crime,
Has this goodbye just woken up?
The sleeping hands of time.

****

Telling Bree

Sit down mother, I've done the sums.
don't get in a lather,
My life does not add up I see,
Frank is not my father.

Is that why we're in Scotland,
Don't you tell me lies?
You went astray, you cheated,
Do you have some big surprise!

I do not want to meet him,
So, get that from your head,
I only have one daddy, Frank.
You seem glad he's dead!

You seem to be deluded,
About your phantom Scot,
People can't go back in time,
He's either dead, or not!

Stop mentioning Culloden,
I'm sure you fantasise,
About this great big highlander,
With red hair and blue eyes.

She was angry with her mother,
That day I broke the news,
I took her settled life apart,
she was so confused.

Had I had some other life,
Compiled some fantasy,
Run off with another man.
Result of which, was she?

Roger made her listen,
He forced me to explain.
They found I was not raving mad,
But actually, quite sane.

Her eyes light when she talks of him.
Sharper than a laser,
She draws a picture of my dad,
A man called Jamie Fraser.

Apparently, I look like him,
Well, I'm not a lot like Frank,
For my Amazonian looks
I have this man to thank.

She says I'll never meet him,
Believes he is long dead,
Deep below Culloden field,
With peat moss at his head.

She says she came to say goodbye.
She will not chase a ghost,
I know that we can find him.
This man she loved the most.

And there he is in writing,
In the records of time,
Years after Culloden,
In prison for his crime.

My mother will go back to him.
I know she'd give her life,
To spend her time beside him
And hear him call her wife.

****

The Mending Basket

I'm not much for mending,
But it must be done,
Walking round in holy socks,
Isn't that much fun,

In my sewing basket
I've the tools to do the task,
Granny Claire what's in there.
Do I hear you ask?

Pins – hold things together.
Until they're really sewn,
Patches – to match everything.
That you'll ever own.

Needles – for my stitching,
Hmm - some I've used on skin,
For sewing up yer grand da,
To keep his innards in.

Thread – very important
It needs to be strong,
Sewing done with rotten thread
Will not last for long.

Wool – for knitting stockings
And darning up your socks,
When you've made big holes in them
Climbing on the rocks.

Ribbon – several colours,
For lacing in your hair,
Making it look pretty.
Or tidy – if you care.

I have another mending kit.
It's much more exciting.
It's my surgeons travelling bag.
I take when there is fighting.

✳✳✳✳

Surgeons Kit

Pass me down that leather roll,
I'll show you what's inside,
That's my surgeons travelling kit.
I pack it when we ride.

There's all the things that I might need.
When we are at war,
Grand Da won't leave me behind,
He lost me once before.

So, I travelled with the men,
When I was in my prime
I trained as a surgeon.
Before I travelled back in time.

Scalpels – make incisions.
Cutting through the skin,
Forceps – for removing things,
Better out than in.

A pot of threaded needles,
Sterilised and ready,
For stitching wounds in battle,
You need a hand that's steady.

See that precious box just there,
That contains syringes,
For injecting penicillin,
Never mind the whinges.

I've used it on your Grand Da,
When he was infected,
I've jabbed that needle in his bum,
Even if he objected.

And then there are my bone saws.
To use for amputation
And irons for the fire
For cauterisation.

I can hear ye Sassenach,
I sense your eyes are gleaming.
Mending human beings
Is the stuff that sets you dreaming.

Watch yer Granny children,
She trained up as which,
I really should'a had her burned,
Before she made one stitch.

****

The Blue Vase

Who would I put into that vase,
Assuming I had bought it,
A dream of having hearth and home,
I never would have thought it.

If it stood upon my mantel shelf,
Above life's burning embers,
What would I give it to contain?
The things that I remember.

Uncle Lamb – where are you now,
You taught me many things,
How to survive when times are hard,
And the knowledge history brings,

Frank – you were my first love,
But you just couldn't see,
Living as professor's wife,
Was not the life for me,

Brianna – oh my daughter,
You are the brightest and the best,
Though your Fraser temper
Still puts me to the test.

Roger – love my daughter,
Don't let her be alarmed!
And look after the children.
Keep them all unharmed!

Rupert - oh and Angus
And of course, there's Ned,
They saved my life more than once,
Without them I'd be dead.

Murtagh – I will miss you.
More than you will know,
Did I ever see you smile?
You never let one show.

Lord John – you are a gentle soul.
Sensitive and kind,
A good friend in a crisis,
An educated mind.

All these would go into my vase,
Memories to treasure,
The people that I love the best,
I could list them forever.

There's one I have forgotten!
I hear you cry out loud,
But I could not put the last one,
In there with the crowd.

A love I could not fathom,
A love that crosses time,
A love so deep it frightens me,
Is such love a crime?

A man of strength and honour,
A man who keeps his word,
A man who saw into my soul,
His vision never blurred.

I trod the winding path I took,
I chose it after all.
Are there regrets – no I have none,
I've answered all life's call.

I have loved, and I love still.
And my love it is returned,
My body is still living.
Not quite beaten up or burned.

I carry him inside my heart.
He lives within my soul,
I would not try and put him.
In any form of bowl

The vase is full of memories.
It is a sort of bank.
If I put Jamie in there.
He might just kill off Frank.

A Final Dream

Last night I dreamed I saw your face.
Hovering above,
You looked so sad it broke my heart.
What's ailing you my love?

I know you're watching over me.
In the time that I have left,
Don't fret so, it will be soon,
Do not feel bereft.

I hanker for the comfort,
Of your arms around.
I miss your body close to me,
To keep me safe and sound.

My bones are old as yours were too,
My spirit young and free,
Let me say my life's goodbyes.
Then I'll fly to thee.

You left me for 200 years.
But watch me all the time,
Kept me safe inside your soul,
As I keep you in mine.

Do not weep, do not be sad.
Soon we'll be together,
We both will guard the young folks.
Playing in the heather.

Time is the great healer,
But now it's time I go.
And join the soul of one I love.
200 years ago.

****

Forget me Not

When my body is no more
My bones are in the earth.
Part of me will live with you,
Forever at your hearth.

I'm with you when you first awake,
Before your eyes adjust
A shadow in the half light,
You'll find me if you must.

When you go about your day to day
When your soul is bare
When you feel life is all too much
Then I will be there,

You'll breath in and you'll smell me.
If you can't quite see
The shadow in the corner
Don't be scairt, it's only me.

When the evening comes around,
You sit upon the porch.
And tell me all about your day,
I'm listening of course.

Listening attentively
As you tell your story
But I was still there with you,
Even though I've gone to glory.

And I will lie beside you.
As you lay your head
Your pillow won't be lonely.
With me inside your head,

Blue flowers on the hillside
In your dreams a Scot.
Make sure you don't forget me.
I will forget you not.

✳✳✳✳

My Worn-out Warrior.

My Jamie is a raconteur,
He loves to tell a story.
He does not spare the detail.
The results can be quite gory,

He tells them all our history.
Sitting round the fire,
He's even shown them all the scars,
Not something to admire,

Their Grand da is their hero.
They treasure every word,
But if he thinks they'll get to sleep
He really is absurd,

The boys are fighting battles.
Sword and dirk in hand,
The girls are fighting with them.
They're all in Grand Da's Clan.

So, I'll leave the warring clansmen.
Until it's time for bed,
I'll listen to his stories.
While I bake the bread.

He could sit there for hours,
Weans wrapped up in his claims.
Enthralling them with stories,
Painting pictures in the flames

I sometimes sit beside him,
Head upon his knee,
And wonder if he's told them.
Of the day that he met me.

Tonight, I'm only fit for bed,
I won't interrupt his flow,
He's getting to a good bit,
I can feel the tension grow,

They'll ask for one more story,
Before they go to bed,
Then my worn-out warrior
May come and rest his head.

Less of the Worn out! Sassenach,
As up the stairs you creep,
I've not lost all my faculties.
To bed now! – not to sleep.

✷✷✷✷

Thank You
For Your Support of
Riding For the Disabled
Best Regards
Maggie J

Copyright: Maggie J 2021

~ 153 ~

Made in United States
North Haven, CT
02 December 2021

11869615R00093